B.T. Clabby

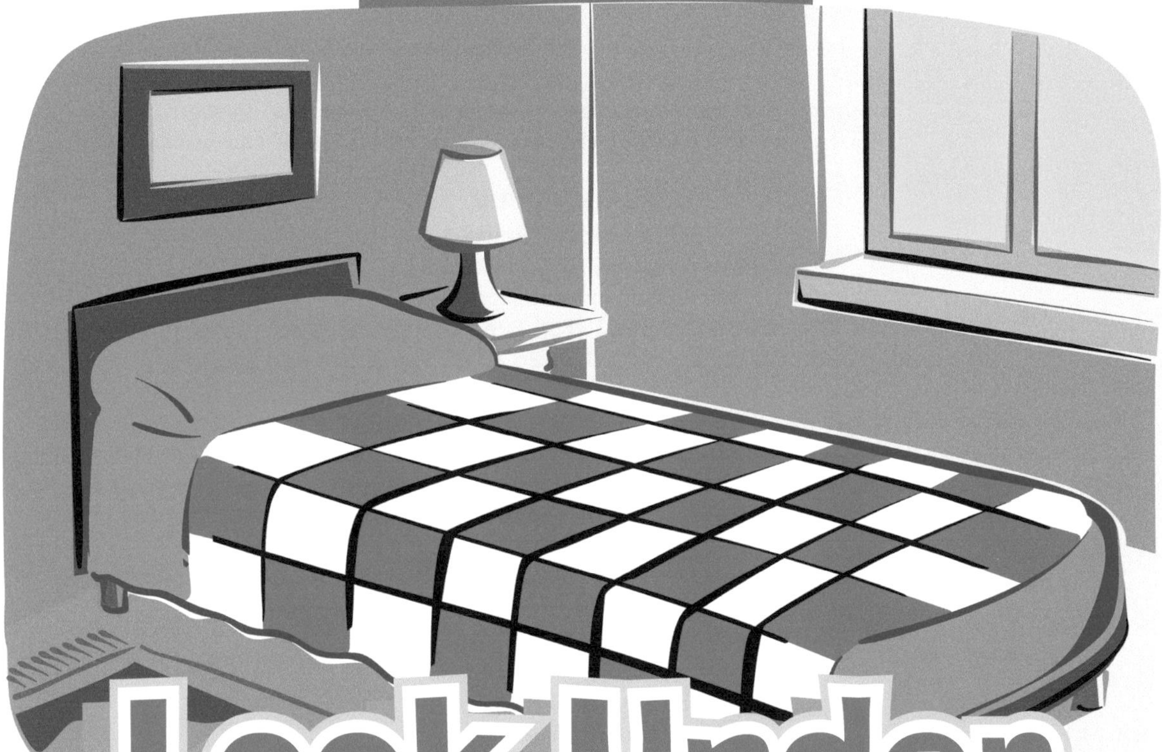

Look Under the BED

AuthorHouse™ UK
1663 Liberty Drive
Bloomington, IN 47403 USA
www.authorhouse.co.uk
UK TFN: 0800 0148641 (Toll Free inside the UK)
UK Local: 02036 956322 (+44 20 3695 6322 from outside the UK)

Because of the dynamic nature of the Internet, any web addresses or links contained in this book may have changed since publication and may no longer be valid. The views expressed in this work are solely those of the author and do not necessarily reflect the views of the publisher, and the publisher hereby disclaims any responsibility for them.

Any people depicted in stock imagery provided by Getty Images are models, and such images are being used for illustrative purposes only. Certain stock imagery © Getty Images.

ISBN: 978-1-6655-9694-7 (sc)
978-1-6655-9695-4 (e)

Published by AuthorHouse 03/15/2022

authorHOUSE®

Look Under the BED

Tomorrow is a special day for Jeremy. It is his first day going into the first grade at school so no longer a little kid, no longer a kindergarten baby. Being as it was so special, Jeremy had to be sure everything was just right so the night before, he got all his new clothes carefully laid out ready for the morning.

The next morning, Jeremy got up already for school. He went to put on his new favorite Toronto Raptors shirt but when he reached over for it, it was gone!?

"Mom I can't find my raptor's shirt," he called down to his mom.

"Look under your Bed," his mother replied.

Jeremy looked down the side of his bed to the floor, then decided to go to the closet to get another shirt.

Then he went to put on his Toronto FC shorts but they were gone?

"Mom I can't find my Toronto FC shorts," he called down

"Look under your Bed," his mother replied.

Jeremy was now a few feet away from his bed and he eyed it suspiciously, however got a new pair of shorts from his drawer.

Then he looked for his Toronto Maple Leaf socks but didn't see them.

"Mom, I can't find my Maple Leaf socks?"

"Look under your Bed" came mom's reply.

Jeremy went over to his sock drawer and found another pair.

Then he went to put on his brand-new running shoes, the type that lights up when you walk in them. But they were gone.

"Mom. I can't find my new running shoes," whined Jeremy.

"Look under your Bed!" mom shouted back.

Jeremy went to his shoe rack and got another older pair of shoes. These ones didn't light up.

Jeremy looked for his autographed Blue Jays baseball cap, but it was nowhere to be found.

"Mom, I can't find my Blue Jays Baseball cap," Jeremy wailed.

"Look under your Bed!" mom answered back.

Jeremy took another cap two sizes too small out of his closet.

Mom can see the school bus coming up the street.

"The bus is coming!" Mom call to the children.

Janice walked past Jeremy's room and looked

in but didn't see her little brother.

"Mom I can't find Jeremy," Janice calls.

"Look under his Bed" is Mom's reply.

The End

About the Book

Jeremy is about to start the first grade and with excitement chooses and puts out his clothes for the day. The next morning, he awakes to find none of his clothes are where he remembers putting them. Is it the dreaded dust bunnies under his bed?

Printed in the United States
by Baker & Taylor Publisher Services